SCAREDY BATH

For Hame, thank you for ensuring our children have
never had a dull bath in their life—Zoë

For my sister, Lauren, who is no longer afraid of bath time—Daniel

PENGUIN WORKSHOP
An imprint of Penguin Random House LLC, New York

First published in Australia by Puffin Books, an imprint of
Penguin Random House Australia Pty Ltd, 2021

First published in the United States of America by Penguin Workshop,
an imprint of Penguin Random House LLC, New York, 2022

Text copyright © 2021 by Zoë Foster Blake
Illustrations copyright © 2021 by Daniel Gray-Barnett

Visit us online at penguinrandomhouse.com.

Library of Congress Cataloging-in-Publication Data is available.

Manufactured in China

ISBN 9780593520635   10 9 8 7 6 5 4 3 2 1 HH

SCAREDY BATH

BY ZOË FOSTER BLAKE
ILLUSTRATED BY DANIEL GRAY-BARNETT

Penguin Workshop

Scaredy Bath was terrified of bath time.
Being a bath, this was a bit of a problem.

Scaredy Bath spent all day . . .

worrying about the evening.

Then Scaredy Bath would hear them coming . . .

shouting . . .

crashing . . .

the stairs.

up

thumping

Sometimes Scaredy Bath was sure
they'd forgotten about bath time.

But they'd always come in the end.

And so the horror would begin.

First came the piping hot water.
Then the gooey soap and the toys.

And, finally,
in came the little ones,
covered in spaghetti and
dirt and smells.

They'd **yank** the plug!
They'd **whack** the tap!
They'd **thrash** and **slide**!
They'd even pee in the water!

Scaredy Bath had a
terrible time, every time.

Just when Scaredy Bath thought it couldn't get any worse,
a new noise came up the stairs.

It was the hairy one!

Scaredy Bath had had enough, once and for all.

It tried to lift its fancy brass feet and run . . .
but they were stuck to the floor!

Was there no end to this
NIGHTMARE?

The sink spoke up.
"Bath time's here to stay, friend.
Might as well try to enjoy it."

The toilet grumbled.
"Think about what I have to put up with."

So Scaredy Bath decided to try and be brave.

The next day Scaredy Bath waited . . .

and waited.

But they didn't come that evening.

Or the one after that.

Or the one after that.

Instead of feeling relieved, Scaredy Bath was . . . bored.
And a bit sad. Were they EVER coming back?

Finally, Scaredy Bath heard them coming . . .

shouting . . .

crashing . . .

thumping up the stairs.

The little ones ran straight in.
They were tanned from the sun, covered in sand,
and smelled like sunscreen and sticky Popsicles.
"YIPEEEE! BATH TIME!" they said, gleefully,
tossing in their toys.

Scaredy Bath was delighted.

Being a bath was fun now . . .

Most of the time.

One day, Scaredy Bath heard a new noise coming up the stairs.

It was a tiny one!

So small, so sweet!

At last, bath time would be gentle and calm.
There'd be nothing to worry about with
something so teeny.

Author photograph copyright © Dave Wheeler

Zoë Foster Blake is the author of this book, and she hopes you love it as much as her kids love peeing in the bath. She is also the author of *No One Likes a Fart*, *No One Likes a Burp*, and one that has no farts or burps in it at all (weird!) called *Go Back to Sleep*.

Daniel Gray-Barnett likes to think of himself as someone who was put on this planet to tell a few stories before he turns into a grumpy old man. He's worked with clients including Disney, Kiehl's, Sydney Opera House, and the *New York Times*, and his first picture book, *Grandma Z*, won a Children's Book Council of Australia Award for Best New Illustrator.